Postman Pat

The Mystery Thief

Story by **John Cunliffe**
Pictures by **Celia Berridge**

from the original Television designs by Ivor Wood

Hippo

Scholastic Children's Books,
7-9 Pratt Street, London NW1 OAE UK
A division of Scholastic Publications Ltd
London - New York - Toronto - Sydney - Auckland

First published in hardback by André Deutsch Limited, 1981
This edition published in the UK by Scholastic Publications Ltd, 1995

ISBN 0 590 13256 3

Printed by Mateu Cromo, S.A. Pinto (Madrid)

Typeset by Rapid

10 9 8 7 6 5 4 3 2 1

Pat was hurrying along the road in his van. Over a hill and round a corner, he had to jam his brakes on, because the road was full of sheep.

Jess popped his head out to have a look. A big ram pushed up to the van, right in Jess's face! What a fright they both had! Peter Fogg was driving his sheep across the road.

He opened a gate, and the sheep went into the field, baa-ing and following their leader. Peter waved as he fastened the gate and Pat went on his way.

Pat soon had to stop again – this time for a herd of cows. They walked slowly by. Mr. Thompson was walking behind them. He waved his stick, and shouted, "Get up, then!" but it made no difference; the cows mooed, stopped to munch the roadside grasses, and took their time.

The road was clear at last.

Mr. Thompson waved to Pat, and Pat was on his way again.

Pat stopped at the village school.

"What lovely flowers," he said to Charlie Pringle.

"They're for our spring display," said Charlie. " Look, here comes Lucy – and Katy and Tom."

They all had something special. Lucy Selby had brought a basket of eggs and Tom Pottage a box of day-old chicks. Bill Thompson brought a cup of tea for Pat and collected the letters.

Then Pat was off again, away up the steep hills and winding roads. In and out of farmyards he went, delivering cards, and letters, and parcels. There was a packet of medicines for Mr. Forsyth, the vet, and a letter about the football pools, for George Lancaster.

"I wonder if he's won," said Pat, but George was out on the fells, so he couldn't ask him. It was almost dinner-time and Pat was near Thompson Ground.

"What a nice place for a picnic," he said. So he parked his van and locked the door. They found a sunny place to sit in the field. Some of Mrs. Thompson's hens were scratching about along the hedges.

Pat could see the Thompsons' farm on the hillside just below where he was sitting. He thought he could almost peep down the chimney and see Mrs. Thompson putting the kettle on the fire.

Jess was thinking about Pat's sandwich-box and hoping there was a tin of sardines in it.

Pat put the box on the grass, with his keys neatly beside it. Jess was in luck: there was a whole tin of sardines to share with Pat, as well as sandwiches, an apple, a yoghurt and a big slice of cherry-cake. It was so warm in the sun that both Pat and Jess began to feel sleepy.

They closed their eyes. Mrs. Thompson's hens were not a bit sleepy. They had spotted Pat's food, too. They pecked their way nearer and nearer to Pat and Jess and the open sandwich box.

A noise wakened Pat. Two hens were running away with sandwiches in their beaks and a third was pecking at the yoghurt. Pat shouted, and chased the hens, but he couldn't catch them. Jess chased another into the hedge. Pat ran back to the sandwich-box just in time to see another cheeky hen running away with his keys in her beak. He chased her down the hill, but she spread her wings and flew into a tree.

"Oh, my keys!" said Pat. "I can't open my van without them! Dear me, it's a long time since I climbed a tree, but I'd better try." Jess glared up at the hen. He could easily climb, but he knew that he couldn't get down again. The cheeky hen sat on a high branch, with the keys in her beak, looking down at Pat and Jess. Pat began to climb, nearer and nearer to the hen.

He was just reaching out to grab the keys, when the hen dropped them into a hollow in the tree and flew off with a loud squawk. Pat put his foot on a rotten branch. Crack! He came tumbling down. He landed in the middle of a prickly bush. It scratched and prickled him all over. Mrs.Thompson came running to see what was going on. She pulled Pat out of the bush and pulled the prickles out of him. He told her all about the thieving hens.

"Dear me," said Mrs. Thompson, "that hen must think she's a magpie; they're the ones for taking anything shiny. We'd better get a ladder and see if we can find your keys."

So they went for the ladder and leaned it against the tree. Pat climbed up easily now. Whilst Mrs. Thompson held the ladder, Pat looked amongst the branches and found the hollow where the hen had dropped the keys. He found a lot of other things there, too.

"It's like a magpie's nest," he said.

He brought it all down to show Mrs. Thompson. There were all kinds of shiny things: bits of glass, wire, a milk-bottle top, buttons, a doll's eye and something larger among the bits and glittery pieces, as well as Pat's keys.

"That's my wedding ring! I thought I'd lost it down the sink," cried Mrs. Thompson. "I'm glad to see it again." She wiped it on her dress and put it on her finger. When they had put the ladder away, she said:

"My hens have stolen your sandwiches, so you'd better come and have some dinner with me – there's plenty to spare."

Pat was glad he'd lost his sandwiches when he saw what a good dinner
Mrs. Thompson had cooked. So was Jess; he had a tasty plate of fish. It was
all much better than the best of sandwiches. Mrs. Thompson was happy, too,
to see her ring shining on her finger once more.

It was time to be on the way and Pat said, "Goodbye," and "Thank you," to Mrs. Thompson. As they drove along, Pat's pocket jingled with all the shiny things he had found in the tree.

"Just fancy," he said, "a magpie-hen. Who ever heard of such a thing?"

Jess wondered what a magpie-cat would collect.

They saw the mobile-shop and Pat stopped to have a chat with Sam. He told him the story of the magpie-hen.

"I wonder if that's where my tie-pin went?" said Sam.

Pat showed him the hen's collection. There were no tie-pins among the glittery bits.

Pat went on his way. He had some letters for Miss Hubbard and he told her about the magpie-hen.

"Well," she said, "I lost a silver earring last month, and a hatpin. I wonder if they're up a tree somewhere? That hen could have another hoard in another tree. I must go and see Mrs. Thompson and have a good look."

Along by Garner Bridge, Pat met George Lancaster and stopped to tell him about the thieving hen. George couldn't think of anything he'd lost, but he thought it made a good story.

"You might have *won* something," said Pat. "There's a letter for you about the pools."

"Is there? I'll be off then," said George.

On the way home, Pat saw some real magpies and wondered if they had taught Mrs. Thompson's hens how to steal. As for Jess, he was asleep.